Please return/renew this item by the last date shown.
Library items may also be renewed by phone on
030 33 33 1234 (24hours) or via our website

www.cumbria.gov.uk/libraries

Cumbria Libraries

CLIC

Interactive Catalogue

Ask for a CLIC password

BY FRANK LAMPARD

THE ELF EXPRESS
FRANK LAMPARD

LITTLE, BROWN BOOKS FOR YOUNG READERS
www.lbkids.co.uk

LITTLE, BROWN BOOKS FOR YOUNG READERS

First published in Great Britain in 2016 by Hodder and Stoughton

1 3 5 7 9 10 8 6 4 2

A CIP catalogue record for this book
is available from the British Library.

ISBN 978-1-51020-111-8

Typeset in Cantarell by M Rules
Printed and bound in Great Britain by
Clays Ltd, St Ives plc

The paper and board used in this book are made
from wood from responsible sources.

MIX
Paper from
responsible sources
FSC® C104740

Little, Brown Books for Young Readers
An imprint of
Hachette Children's Group
Part of Hodder and Stoughton
Carmelite House
50 Victoria Embankment
London EC4Y 0DZ

An Hachette UK Company
www.hachette.co.uk

www.hachettechildrens.co.uk

*To my mum Pat, who encouraged me to
do my homework in between kicking
a ball all around the house, and is still
with me every step of the way.*

*Welcome to a fantastic
Fantasy League – the greatest
football competition ever held
in this world or any other!*

*You'll need four on a team,
so choose carefully. This is a lot
more serious than a game in the
park. You'll never know who your
next opponents will be, or
where you'll face them.*

*So lace up your boots, players,
and good luck! The whistle's
about to blow!*

The Ref

PART ONE

CHAPTER 1

Frankie wheeled his arms, trying to keep his balance. Louise slid past, her snowboard cutting through the powdery snow.

"You're doing great!" she said. "Just don't lean back."

"And keep your knees bent," called Charlie, whizzing down the slope with his ski poles tucked under his arm.

Frankie managed to stay on his skis and shuffled forward.

I'm doing it! he thought. *This isn't so hard ...*

"And get out of my way!" yelled Kevin.

Frankie felt something slam into his shoulder and spin him round. He landed with a thump in the snow in time to see his brother skiing past.

"Oops! Sorry, Frankenstein," cackled Kevin.

Frankie took a deep breath of the cold mountain air. Skiing was tough! The fact that Kevin was really good at it made it even more annoying.

Frankie's Austrian friend Heidi brought herself to a halt at his side. "Your brother's not very nice, is he?" she said. "Up you stand, Frankie."

Frankie clambered to his feet, and brushed the snow off his ski suit. "I'm hopeless," he said.

"Not true," Heidi replied. "It's like riding a bicycle – soon it will be easy. Come on, I will stay with you."

Frankie turned his skis and began to slide down slowly. They'd been in Austria for three days, staying with his pen pal Heidi and her family. So far all he'd managed to do was fall over. It was his first time skiing, but it was new to Charlie too and he wasn't having any problems. Still, it was great being away with his friends and doing something different.

"Be loose," said Heidi at his side. "You look very stiff and tense."

"That's because I'm bruised all over," laughed Frankie.

He began to pick up speed. Right towards a tree.

"OK, lean left," said Heidi.

Frankie did as she said, and steered back towards the centre of the slope.

"Don't look at your feet," said Heidi. "Look ahead."

Frankie gazed at the view beyond – huge mountains covered in snow and pine forests and dotted with chalets. Ski lifts and cable cars full of people drifted across the white expanse.

"Go, Frankie!" said Louise, as he skied past her.

Frankie realised he hadn't fallen over for a while. *Perhaps I'm finally getting it.*

They were here for a whole week over Christmas, staying at Heidi's chalet, so he still had lots of chances to improve. The slopes were even open on Christmas Day. As Frankie drifted to a halt at the bottom of the run, Charlie was waiting with a raised glove.

"Nice work!" he said.

Frankie high-fived him, grinning.

There was a café at the bottom of the run. Inside, Heidi's older brother Marc was drinking a coffee. He was a professional ski instructor.

Louise skidded to a halt next to Frankie. "Fancy one more go?" she said.

Heidi pointed with a ski pole to the sky, where Frankie spotted a thick grey cloud coming over a ridge. "We need to go home soon," she said. "The forecast says we will have a storm later."

"That storm's ages away," said Kevin. "I'm going up again."

He was already clambering into a ski-lift chair.

Heidi's brother emerged, putting on his jacket. "Time to head back to the house," he said.

Heidi pointed to Kevin. "All right. We will get him and hurry home."

Easy for you to say, thought Frankie. *I can only go so fast.*

"OK," said Marc. "But stick to the easy slope."

They climbed on to the lift. Most of the other people were heading

off the slopes, Frankie noticed.
It was Christmas Eve, after all,
and they were probably going
to get warm and cosy by their
fires. Frankie's parents had been
decorating the Christmas tree at
the chalet with Heidi's mum and
dad.

As they rose, Frankie saw the
distant cloud more clearly. It was
moving fast on high winds. He
shivered. The mountains were
incredible, but Heidi's brother loved
telling stories about all the things
that could go wrong – white-outs,
avalanches and frostbite.

By the time they reached the top

of the green run again, Frankie's fingers and toes were cold, and the sun was hidden by cloud. "Let's make this quick," he said.

"I'm doing the black run," said Kevin. He stayed on the lift as it climbed higher.

"That's silly, Kev," called Frankie. So far they'd just been on the green piste, which was the easiest. Black runs were for experienced skiers.

"I had better go with him," said Heidi, clambering back on to the lift. "See you all at the bottom?"

Frankie nodded. They were lucky they had Heidi with them – she'd been skiing since before she could walk.

He, Louise and Charlie lined up at the top of the slope. "I'm looking forward to a hot chocolate," said Charlie, flexing his goalie gloves on the top of his ski poles.

"Didn't you fancy wearing proper ski gloves?" asked Louise.

Charlie looked at her as if she was mad, and Louise grinned. They all knew Charlie never took off his goalie gloves, even though a game of football looked unlikely three thousand metres up an icy mountain.

"Let's go!" said Frankie, edging off.

This time he reached the bottom without falling over once. Louise and Charlie clapped their hands.

"I wonder how Heidi and Kevin are doing?" said Frankie, peering further up the mountain.

"We can't just stand around," said Louise, stepping off her board. "It's too cold. Let's head to the bottom of the black run to meet them."

They clipped off their hire skis, and handed them in at the café. Frankie shouldered his rucksack. They walked through the snow and arrived at the black run just in time to see Kevin sliding down on his

back, skis at an angle. He bumped
into the barrier with a groan. Heidi
swished to a halt beside him.

"What happened?" asked Frankie.
"Are you OK?"

Kevin grimaced through a face-
full of snow. "Twisted my ankle," he
said, blushing.

"What a surprise," grumbled Charlie.

"You could have been badly hurt!" said Heidi. She looked more annoyed than Frankie had ever seen her. He felt embarrassed. *Why can't Kevin just behave himself?*

The sky darkened suddenly as the cloud swept overhead. Snow swirled around, thick and fast, and the ski lifts clanked. Heidi looked worried.

"We don't have time to return to the chalet," she said. "My grandfather has a cabin a little way down the mountain. We can shelter there until the storm has gone over."

"Mum and Dad will be worried," said Frankie.

"It's OK – there's a phone," said Heidi. "Storms here can be very bad. We must stay safe."

Supporting Kevin between them, they trudged down the mountainside. The snow continued to fall heavily and a wind gusted through the trees.

"Not much further now," said Heidi.

It was already hard to see more than twenty or thirty metres ahead, and off the main slope the snow was so thick Frankie kept sinking over his ankles. He heard a rumble of thunder from the sky. Or was it an avalanche? He peered at the mountaintops, but they were hidden by clouds.

I hope Heidi can get us out of this.

CHAPTER 2

"There!" said Louise.

Frankie glimpsed the outline of a cabin through the snowfall. *We're safe!*

Heidi found a key under a flowerpot on the windowsill and opened the door. They all hurried in, shaking the snow off their clothes. Frankie looked around. The cabin was one large room, with thick rugs, a bed in the corner, and a wood-burning stove. It was freezing, but at least it was out of the howling wind. For a moment, Frankie had a pang of missing his dog, Max. Normally, there would always be a bark of welcome when Frankie walked through the front door, but they'd had to leave him back in England with Frankie's grandparents. He'd be stuffed full of leftovers and snoozing on the sofa by now.

"How long do you think the storm will last?" asked Kevin. His breath formed clouds on the air.

Heidi looked out of the windows

with a frown. "I do not know. You should rest your foot."

As Kevin settled on to the bed, she went to an ancient-looking phone, picked up the receiver and dialled. Frankie knew mobiles didn't work this side of the mountain. Then she spoke in German with someone at the other end.

"My parents were just starting to worry," she said when she had finished the call, "but they will tell your mum and dad we are here. They say the storm will be gone in maybe two hours, and Marc will come over when it's safe."

The wind howled outside.

"Is this place sturdy?" asked Kevin.

Heidi chuckled. "It's been here sixty years – it will take more than a little storm to damage it."

"As long as we're not stuck here for Christmas Day," said Charlie, taking off his boots. He kept his gloves on, as always.

"We will make it cosy," said Heidi. She began to pile small sticks and rolls of scrap newspaper into the stove, then put in a couple of logs. She struck a match and lit it. Soon the little stove was throwing out waves of lovely heat. Frankie peeled off his coat.

"I'm hungry!" said Kevin. "Don't suppose you've any food in that bag of yours, Frankie?"

Frankie's rucksack was by the door. "'Fraid not," he said.

"So what *is* in there?" asked Charlie.

25

Frankie smiled. "Just warm clothes," he said. The truth was that he'd brought the magic football with him on holiday. He liked to keep it close, at all times.

Kevin was sulking as he inspected his ankle. It did look a bit swollen.

Heidi opened a cupboard. Inside Frankie saw tins of soup and packets of biscuits. She took out a bag.

"Marshmallows!" said Louise.

Soon they were toasting their marshmallows by the stove fire. Using milk powder, they made cups of hot chocolate too. In a chest under the table, Frankie found a pack of cards and several board games.

They played a game as the snow mounted up against the windows.

"This isn't so bad," said Charlie.

They all jumped at the sound of a bang outside. "What was that?" said Kevin.

"I think it is just a shutter," said Heidi.

"It might have been a yeti," said Charlie.

"Yetis aren't real, silly," said Louise. "And anyway, they're supposed to be in the Himalayas, not the Alps."

"Maybe it's on a skiing holiday too," laughed Frankie. He looked at his watch. They'd been cooped up for nearly three hours and it was getting dark outside.

"I think we will be spending the night here," said Heidi, peering out of the window. "What a shame we will not see the tree until tomorrow."

"I meant to ask," said Frankie. "Why do you only decorate your trees on Christmas Eve?"

"It is a tradition," said Heidi. "It is bad luck to see the Christmas tree before it is dark on Christmas Eve. Mum says it's to stop us eating the *vanillekipferl*."

"The what?" said Charlie.

"Vanilla biscuits," said Heidi. "We hang them on the tree."

"Weird," said Kevin.

"We think your mince pies are weird," said Heidi.

"Then what do you leave out for Santa?" asked Charlie.

"We do not have Santa Claus or Father Christmas," said Heidi.

"So who brings your presents?" asked Charlie, looking alarmed.

"The Christmas elves," said Heidi. "They come when we are all asleep and put sweets in our shoes."

"Yeah, sure," said Kevin, with a snort. "I bet it's just your parents."

"Maybe," said Heidi, shrugging.

By the time they'd finished their card game, Kevin was snoring.

Louise's eyes were drooping, too.

"Let's get some rest," Frankie said, relaxing into the armchair.

Heidi found some blankets in the chest and gave one to each of them. Then she curled up on the battered sofa.

Charlie climbed on to the bed, so that he was top to tail with Kevin. He wrinkled his nose at Kevin's socks.

Frankie listened to the crackle of the logs in the stove. *Tomorrow will be Christmas Day*, he thought. He couldn't help but feel a tingle of excitement, but his eyelids were growing heavier and heavier . . .

*

He woke to a scratching sound. Sitting up, Frankie looked around the dark room. The others were still asleep, and the logs were embers in the stove. Frankie shivered. Outside, the snow had stopped falling.

More scratching. Frankie stretched and stood up.

Where's it coming from?

He found the matches, and lit one of the candles. Light flared across the cabin.

Something moved, scurrying under the cupboards.

"A mouse?" said Frankie.

Louise stirred, yawning. "What time is it?"

Frankie checked his watch. "Just after midnight!" he said.

One by one the others woke as well. Heidi reached for the phone. "I will tell my parents we are all OK . . . oh!" Her brow creased. "The phone line is down."

"Must be the storm," said Charlie.

Frankie crouched down, looking under the cupboard. "I thought I saw a mouse," he said. There was nothing underneath, though.

"OK, who's playing tricks?" said Kevin. He pointed to their shoes by the door. To Frankie's surprise, he saw they were all filled with sweets in brightly coloured wrappers. "Who put them there?" said Frankie's brother.

"It must be the elves," said Heidi.

"Yeah, right," said Kevin, rolling his eyes.

"What's under there, then?" cried Louise, pointing at the far corner of the room. One of Frankie's boots seemed to be trembling. All around it, the floor sparkled with something like gold glitter.

Frankie tiptoed over, and picked up the boot by its sole. Everyone gasped. Crouching underneath was a boy.

A tiny boy, less than fifteen centimetres tall.

"A Christmas elf!" said Heidi.

CHAPTER 3

"Quick, squash it!" said Kevin. He picked up another shoe.

"No!" yelled Frankie.

The elf ran through his legs and under the sofa, leaving a trail of gold dust.

"You've frightened him," said Louise, scowling at Kevin.

"It's all right!" said Frankie. "We won't hurt you."

The elf stuck his head out. "Promise?"

Frankie nodded, and narrowed his eyes at his brother. Kevin dropped the shoe. "Are you really an elf?" Frankie asked.

"That's right," said the elf, puffing out his chest.

Frankie rubbed his eyes. *Is this real?*

"So what are you doing here?" asked Charlie.

The elf spread his hands. "I fell off the back of our sledge. When I managed to climb out of the snow, it had disappeared. I need to get home, but the snow's too thick."

"We'll help you," Frankie said. "I'm Frankie, by the way."

"Gustav," said the elf, holding out his hand. Frankie extended his little finger and they shook.

Louise and the others introduced themselves.

"So, how can you get home?" said Heidi.

"We go to the crossing place," said Gustav. "I can show you the way, but we have to be quick."

Frankie and his friends began to put on their boots, but Kevin remained where he was. "I think we should stay put," he said. "How do you know you can trust this little goblin thing?"

"He's an *elf*," said Frankie. "And why shouldn't we believe him?"

"Well, I'm not going anywhere," said his brother, folding his arms. "My ankle still hurts."

"Fine," said Frankie, pulling on his coat and rucksack. No way was he leaving his brother alone with the magic football. "Stay here if that's what you want." He held out his hand to Gustav. "Want a lift?"

"Thanks!" said the elf, stepping into his palm. Frankie tucked him carefully in his pocket.

"Watch out for yetis!" said Kevin. When they opened the door, snow had piled up against it. Fresh recent falls weighed down the tree branches and covered the ground in pillowy drifts. Though it was night, the bright moon made everything glow.

"Which way?" asked Frankie, sinking up to his ankles in the snow.

Gustav pointed downhill. "Head that way," he said. "It isn't far."

They trudged out of the cabin, following his directions. It was really tough going and soon Frankie was breathing hard. Gustav didn't lead them in a straight line, but directed them to veer left and right among trees as if he wasn't quite

sure which way to go. At one point
Frankie even thought they'd gone in
a circle. He glanced over at Louise,
who arched her eyebrow. Charlie
stumbled into a snowdrift.

"Are you sure about this,
Gustav?" he said, brushing snow
off his gloves.

"Yes, yes," said the elf. "Almost there now."

Frankie was just starting to lose hope when Gustav gasped.

"Oh no!" He pointed at a set of tracks in the snow.

"What's the matter?" asked Frankie.

Gustav pointed at the two lines, just a few centimetres apart. They led to the edge of the cliff.

"They've gone home without me!" he said.

Frankie's heart skipped a beat. The drop from the cliff edge was thousands of metres high. Far below, in the distance, the lights

of a town twinkled in the valley.
"What — down there?"

Gustav shook his head sadly. "Elf
magic takes us home to our world,"
he said. His shoulders slumped.
"I'm stuck here. They won't come
back for another year!"

Frankie looked at his friends. He
felt dreadful. It was one thing to
be trapped overnight by a storm,
but poor Gustav would be stuck
here until next Christmas. Heidi
shrugged. There was really nothing
they could do.

Unless . . .

Frankie shrugged off his
rucksack, and unzipped it.

"I might have a way," he muttered, taking out the magic football.

"I don't think a game of football will help now," said Heidi.

"There's a bit more to it than that," said Charlie.

Frankie took a deep breath. He set the football on the ground and took a step back.

"What are you going to do?" said Louise.

"We need magic, right?" said Frankie. "Well, the football's never let us down before."

"That football doesn't look very magical," said Heidi. "It looks sort of . . . burst."

Frankie smiled. *I hope this works.*

Drawing back his foot, he kicked the ball over the edge of the cliff.

Charlie gasped, and Louise let out a yelp. Frankie watched the ball rise into the night air, then drop out of sight.

"I think you have just lost your old football," said Heidi.

Charlie sighed. "Nice try, Frankie."

Frankie's heart sank. "I thought it—"

"Look!" cried Louise, pointing into the sky. "There's something up there!"

She was right. A golden dot glimmered in the distance, like a bright star. And it was getting bigger by the second. Gustav hopped up and down in excitement. "I think you have done it!" he said. "The Elf Express — it's here!"

As the light grew, Frankie saw it was shaped like a large telephone box, drifting steadily closer, its sides glittering.

"It's a cable car!" said Charlie.

Frankie grinned. The car didn't seem to be suspended from a cable, though — it was floating on thin air.

With a creaking sound, it came to a halt in front of them,

settling in the snow. It was made of rusting metal and old wooden panels, open to the elements, with a simple door that came up to Frankie's waist. A sharp yap came from inside the cable car and there was a patter of claws across the floorboards as . . .

"Max!" Frankie cried. His magic football must have brought his pet dog all the way to Austria. He ran inside the cable car, with the others following behind.

As Max leapt into Frankie's arms and licked his face, Louise looked around.

"It looks about a hundred years

old!" she said. "Are you sure it's safe?"

"Oh yes!" said Gustav. But before he could say anything else, the cable car lurched sideways and they all fell into each other. The football rolled across the floor as the cable car began scraping through the snow. Right towards the huge drop.

"Maybe we should get off?" said Charlie. He tried the door which had slammed shut behind them, but it didn't open. "We're trapped!"

They moved closer to the edge of the mountain.

"Don't panic," said Gustav. "It can probably hold your weight."

"Probably?" Max barked, as the cable car slid off the edge of the mountain.

CHAPTER 4

Frankie's whole body felt suddenly light. They were floating! How was that possible?

"See – nothing to worry about," said Gustav. "Now it's only a short ride back to the elf village."

"I think I must be dreaming," said Heidi. "Frankie, you did not mention a magic football in your letters to me. Or a talking dog."

Frankie smiled, putting Max back down. "I didn't think you'd believe me."

"I would not have," said Heidi, grinning back. "I don't think I would have invited a mad English boy to stay for Christmas either."

The Elf Express climbed higher and higher. They entered low-hanging clouds that glowed almost silvery in the moonlight, so thick that Frankie couldn't see a thing outside.

"Elf mist," said Gustav. Frankie, Charlie and Louise shared a silent glance. *Elf mist?*

Frankie wondered how Kevin was

doing back at Heidi's grandfather's cabin. *He's probably finished all the marshmallows by now.*

There was a jolt and the cable car began to head downwards. They picked up speed.

"Er ... is it supposed to go this fast?" Louise asked.

"I don't know," said Gustav.

The cable car clanked and screeched. Frankie saw sparks flying as they shot through the sky.

"I think maybe we should hold on to something," said Heidi.

Frankie noticed Louise's knuckles were white as she gripped the side. He grabbed on, too. Charlie sat down with his head between his knees.

The whole structure rattled and shook. Frankie looked out and saw nothing but mist.

With a thump, the bottom of the cable car hit the ground, and tipped over. Frankie flew through the air, landing face-first on the snow, Max beside him.

He spat out a mouthful of snow and rolled over, groaning.

"Is everyone OK?" he said.

"Yes," said Heidi.

"I think so," said Louise.

"That was quite a landing," muttered Charlie.

Frankie felt a hand grab his wrist, and he blinked to see a boy standing over him. It took a moment to realise it was Gustav, but instead of being tiny, he was normal-sized. And weirder still, the sky was bright. It was somehow daytime.

"Welcome to the elf world," Gustav said, hauling Frankie up.

Frankie looked at his friends picking themselves up off the snow. The cable car was nowhere to be seen, and they were standing on a cliff just like the one they'd left. The football rested beside Frankie, so he picked it up and put

it in his rucksack. *I knew it would work!*

"Wait – you've grown!" said Charlie, brushing the snow off his gloves.

Gustav chuckled. "Not exactly!" he said. "It isn't me who's bigger. You've shrunk!"

Frankie looked down at his body — he was wearing the same clothes, with the same rucksack on his back. He didn't *feel* any different.

"Are you sure?"

Max lifted a paw to inspect it. "This means I must be smaller than a kitten," he growled. "I don't like that at all."

Gustav nodded. "If you had stayed the same size, you would have trampled our village. Come on, I'll show you."

He headed off up a snowy slope.

"How do we get back?" called Charlie.

"We'll talk to the elders," replied Gustav over his shoulder. Then he mumbled something that sounded like "Shouldn't be a problem."

As they reached the crest of the low hill, Frankie saw the lights of a village below, houses clustered around a central square. He heard a shrill whistle.

"Make way, make way!" cried a voice. A sledge rushed through the snow towards them, pulled by dogs and carrying several elves along with a bulging sack. Frankie and the others jumped back as it shot past. Only when it was near did he see

that they weren't dogs at all, but huge white and brown mice, noses twitching.

Gustav waved as it shot off the edge of the cliff and climbed into the sky.

"Another Christmas delivery," he said, like it was the most normal thing in the world.

As they made their way towards the village, a steady stream of sledges passed them, all loaded with sweets.

"I always knew the elves were real!" said Heidi.

The first of the buildings they came to was a picnic hamper

with windows cut in the side, and
Frankie grinned as he realised the
other buildings were all recycled,
too. They were made of tins and
crates and plastic boxes, or domes
made from bowls turned upside-
down.

"It's all rubbish!" said Charlie.

Gustav nodded. "You humans
throw away an awful lot of useful
things," he said. There were several
sets of skis leaning up against an
old biscuit tin. "Let's put these on.
It'll be easier to get around," said
the elf.

On closer inspection, Frankie saw
that the skis were lollipop sticks,

and Gustav gave them all poles
made of cocktail sticks. He was
right, it was much easier getting
over the hard-packed snow using
the skis. They glided along a street,
with fairy lights of every colour
strung between the buildings.
The smells of cooking came from
the houses, and smoke drifted
from chimneys cut into the roofs.
The streets were busy with elves
bustling about, carrying sweets
or chocolates in their wrappers,
loading up sledges. A few glanced
at Frankie and his friends.

*I suppose our ski jackets and
trousers look strange to them.*

"What do you do when it's not Christmas?" asked Louise.

"We make all the sweets in our factories, then there's the mouse stable to look after, sledge maintenance, magic dust preparation, stealth training. It's a full-time job being a Christmas elf," said Gustav.

A group of elf children ran past, throwing snowballs and laughing. "It's not all hard work, though," he added.

A loud clanking noise made Gustav freeze. "Uh-oh," he said.

From around a corner came three rats, each as big as a horse, with bells around their necks. Sitting on their backs were elves wearing black clothes. They spread out, two circling behind Frankie and his friends, one reining to a stop just ahead. The rats snarled, showing jagged teeth, their beady eyes looking at Frankie and his friends.

"Gustav?" said Louise. "Are we safe?"

From the way Gustav was trembling, Frankie wasn't sure.

CHAPTER 5

"Gustav!" said the leader. "Who are these strangers in our village?"

Gustav blushed. "Hello, Hans," he said. "These humans helped me get home."

Hans flinched. "Humans! Don't you know the elf code?"

"I do," said Gustav, "but—"

"Then repeat Elf Rule Number One for me," said the elf.

"Wait!" said Frankie. "It's our fault. There was a cable car and—"

"Silence!" said Hans. Frankie stopped. He didn't like Hans very much so far. "Gustav. Rule Number One, please."

"Elves must do everything possible to avoid contact with humans," said Gustav.

"Does the rule say anything about humans' pets?" Max muttered.

Hans glared at Gustav, then spoke quietly. "You will come with us to the Elders," he said.

Gustav nodded. "What about my friends?" he asked. "They helped me get home!"

Hans glared at Frankie and the others. "The *trespassers* can wait here," he said, "until we decide what to do with them."

Not sure I like the sound of that, thought Frankie.

Hans turned his rat around, and Gustav trailed after them.

"He's not very friendly," said Charlie.

"Maybe we should go home," said Heidi. "Can we use your football, Frankie?"

He took the football out. Frankie wondered if its magic would even work any more.

"I think we should try to talk to

the elf Elders first," he said. "It's not right that Gustav's in trouble because of us."

"I agree," said Louise. "Let's just stay put for now."

A snowball hit Charlie in the back. "Hey!" he said. "Who threw that?"

An elf boy peeped out from behind an empty sledge, grinning.

"Right!" said Charlie, scooping up a handful of snow. He hurled it back, but the boy ducked out of sight. There were more elves gathering. "Snow fight!" one of them called, and soon the snowballs were flying. Frankie almost forgot that they were in a

magical world far from home. Snow
trickled down his back, making him
shudder. Louise's hair was covered,
and Charlie's gloves were caked
with ice. Heidi slipped and the elves
closed in, covering her with snow.

"Truce! Truce!" called Frankie,
laughing. "You win."

The elves stopped and helped Heidi up. Many of them were staring, as if afraid to speak.

"It's OK," said Frankie. "We don't bite."

"We've never seen a real human before," said a young girl. "The Elders told us you were giants."

"We are, I suppose," said Frankie. "Well, we were. But really, we're just like you."

The elf children all giggled. "With weird ears!" one said.

Another one ran past and grabbed the football out of Frankie's hands. "Let's play!" he said, passing the ball to a girl.

Frankie looked across at his friends. "Maybe we've got time for a quick game?" he said.

"Always," Charlie said. The elf girl took a shot and Charlie caught it in his gloves. "You'll have to do better than that to get past me, though."

They separated into two teams, a mixture of elves and humans on each side.

The elves were all quick on their feet, and Frankie soon forgot about going easy on them. The girl managed to score a goal past Charlie.

"Beginner's luck," he muttered, red-faced.

After ten minutes the score was two all, but Frankie remembered Gustav. *We really should find out what's happened to him.*

"Next goal wins," he said.

He passed to Heidi, who managed to dribble past a couple of elves, before being tackled by Louise. Then Louise ran straight at Frankie, stepping over the ball with her quick feet. But Frankie knew all her tricks. As she feinted one way, he stood his ground, and managed to take the ball. He left a defender sprawling, and lined up a shot at the elf keeper. The ball left his foot in a perfect curled shot towards the top corner.

Frankie lifted his arms in triumph. But the elf keeper stood completely still and no one cheered. Charlie cleared his throat and Frankie turned to see that Hans had returned, not on his rat this time, but with several other elves in dark robes. A few of the elf children scurried off between the buildings.

Frankie noticed someone was missing.

"Where's Gustav?" asked Frankie.

"Don't worry about him," said Hans. "He's told us all we need to know."

"When can we go home?" asked Charlie.

Hans shot him a look. "Gustav committed a grave offence by bringing you here. Our world is supposed to be a secret, but somehow you managed to cross using that ball of yours."

Frankie looked back for his ball, but he couldn't see it anywhere.

"Listen, we didn't mean to come here," Frankie said. "I promise we won't tell anyone about the elf world."

"So you say," snapped Hans. "But how can we trust you?"

Frankie didn't know what to say.

"I thought elves were supposed to be nice," said Heidi.

"We need to speak further," said Hans. "You will stay for a few days more while we work out what to do."

"A few days?" said Frankie. "But we need to get home to our parents. They won't know what's happened."

Hans nodded. "That is unfortunate. But the Elders have decided."

"Do you think he'd jump off a cliff if the Elders told him to?" muttered Max.

Hans stared at him, eyes bulging. "That's it! You can go with the other animals. I'm sick of your cheek!"

Before Frankie could do anything, elves rushed forwards and scooped up his dog, marching towards a building that looked like a barn. Max barked frantically back at Frankie, but Hans had gripped his arm.

Frankie stared at his friends. This was turning into a Christmas nightmare!

PART TWO

CHAPTER 6

"Now," said Hans as he led Frankie and his friends away from the square through the elf village, "you can make yourselves useful at the plant."

Frankie could hardly believe what he was hearing. What was the "plant", anyway? And where was his football?

They trudged past the barn with empty sledges parked outside.

The scent of animals came wafting from a set of stable doors. Frankie saw lots of mice peeping out, all squeaking. Was Max in there?

There was a panicked bark he'd have recognised anywhere.

Frankie ran towards the sound and leaned over the stable door. A familiar muzzle poked up.

"Max!" he said. "Are you OK?"

Max growled at a mouse and put his paws on the inside of the door to nuzzle Frankie's hand. "I'll have to be."

"Get away from that dog!" said Hans. "He needs to earn his keep like everyone else."

A couple of elves pulled Frankie
away from the stable doors.

"Don't worry, boy," he called.
"We'll get you out soon."

One by one, the sledges were
being moved in front and mice yoked
up. At the next building, bulging

sacks of sweets were hoisted on to the back of the sledges.

"As you see," said Hans, "this is quite an operation. Everyone has to pull their weight."

He stopped outside the next building and waved them inside. There was the sound of noisy clanking, along with hundreds of singing voices. The air was thick with the sweet smells of sugar and caramel and chocolate. From floor to ceiling, conveyor belts chugged through the huge chamber, carrying sweets. They dropped through gaps, tumbled down rollers, then passed between rows of smiling elves wearing hairnets who inspected them. Then a belt took them to a place where more elves wrapped crinkly paper around the sweets.

"Is anyone else hungry?" said Charlie.

Now they were inside, Frankie could hear the words of the song more clearly.

"A day of joy and presents
    sweet
They never hear our elvish feet
We creep across their bedroom
    floor
And leave our gifts while they
    snore.

Sugar drops, melted chocs,
Fill the children's Christmas
socks."

"You lot will start with wrapping,"
said Hans. "Later I might let you
move to sledge maintenance." He
pointed to a changing room filled
with protective gear like the other
elves were wearing. "Off you go."

"This is a big mistake," said
Heidi.

"The mistake was crossing to the
elf world," said Hans. "And take
those silly gloves off," he added,
glaring at Charlie.

He turned and strode out of the

door, closing it behind him.

"He didn't mean that, did he?" asked Charlie. "About the gloves?"

Louise put her arm around Charlie's shoulder. "You keep them on if you want."

"Let's get to work and get thinking," said Frankie. All the elves seemed to be enjoying their work, but he didn't want to miss Christmas. "There's a way out of this."

There's got to be.

Frankie lost track of time, and of how many sweets he was wrapping. His arms ached worse than if he'd done a thousand press-ups. And still the sweets kept coming. Bonbons, pear drops, chocolates, gobstoppers, cola cubes, fruit gums and pastilles. He managed a smile as he wrapped his mum's favourite, a strawberry sherbet. But he was worried about Max, stuck with all those mice.

Louise tucked a stray lock of hair back under her hairnet. "I never want to see another sweet in my life," she grumbled.

Charlie looked ready to doze off.

"Any plan yet?" asked Heidi. "Perhaps if we beg the Elders . . ."

Frankie sighed. Hans had seemed very stubborn. "I think we're going to have to escape," he said.

"Psst!" said a voice.

Frankie spotted a familiar face poking round the door.

"Gustav! Are you OK?"

The elf scurried over to them, holding a sweet in a red wrapper.

"I'm fine," he said, "just on mouse mucking-out duty for the rest of the week! I'm sorry I got you into trouble, but I've brought you this."

"Er . . . thanks," said Frankie. "But we're really not hungry."

"Open it," whispered Gustav.

Frankie took the sweet and

realised straight away that it wasn't anything edible. It was too light. Peeling back the wrapper, he saw the scuffed leather of the magic football.

"Perfect!" said Frankie. "Now we just need to get to the cliffs."

Gustav shook his head. "You'll never make it back through the village," he said. "You'll be spotted by an Elder, for sure."

"So, how are we getting home?" said Heidi.

Gustav swallowed "There is another way," he said gravely. "The misty lake — straight down the hill away from the village."

"Why do you look so worried?" asked Charlie.

"It's dangerous," said Gustav. "We elves used to go that way every time, when the lake was frozen. These days the ice is thinner."

"We'll risk it," said Frankie. "We have to."

The sound of bells clanking made them all freeze. "It's a patrol!" said Gustav. "I have to go!" He held out his hand. "Good luck, Frankie." Frankie shook his hand, and Gustav rushed for the door. He turned back. "One more thing. When you return to your world, you must eat some of the Christmas biscuit! The ones that hang on the tree. It is the only thing that will make you big again."

"Thank you," said Frankie, but Gustav had already vanished.

"The misty lake it is, then," said Louise. "Now we just have to get out of *here*."

Frankie was eyeing the changing room. "I think I might have a plan," he whispered to the others. He looked around at all the other elves at work. No one seemed to be paying much attention. "If we can disguise ourselves in elf clothes, we might be able to slip away."

"So if we can do that, if we can get to the lake, if we manage to cross the thin ice, *and* if we manage to eat one of the magic biscuits, we'll be all right?" said Charlie.

"Maybe don't say it like that," said Heidi.

Frankie clutched his magic football.

This might be our trickiest mission yet . . .

CHAPTER 7

They managed to sneak from the conveyor belt to the changing room without anyone noticing, dressed in elf clothes made of scraps of old fabric and leaves over their own clothes. At any moment, Frankie expected someone to raise the alarm. Sweets were piling up, ready to be wrapped.

They crept to the doors, and

looked outside. No sign of any rats or helpers, but Frankie could hear the ringing bell somewhere not far off.

Louise touched his shoulder, and pointed towards the mouse stables. "Maybe we could get a ride," she whispered.

Frankie nodded. "We need to blend in and find Max," he said. "Everyone, grab some sweets."

Soon they were trudging towards the stables, all carrying an armful of sweets. They copied the other elves, loading them onto the back of a sledge yoked with eight mice.

"I'll get your dog," muttered

Heidi. She broke away and sneaked through a stable door.

Frankie climbed into the driver's position and picked up the reins. *How long until someone spots us?*

"Hold on a minute!" boomed a familiar voice. "That sledge isn't fully loaded."

Frankie's hopes popped like a burst balloon. Hans.

He didn't want to turn around. There was a chance they could still get away if Hans didn't recognise them.

Frankie waited, heart thumping, as elves stacked more sacks of sweets on the back of the sledge.

From the corner of his eye, he saw that Hans was already inspecting another sledge, barking orders.

"Where are Heidi and Max?" whispered Louise.

Frankie shot a glance at the stable door. *Come on . . .* he willed.

"Wait!" cried Hans. "I know those gloves!"

"Oops!" said Charlie.

Hans was pointing right at them. At the same moment the stable doors behind him burst open and mice flooded out. Hans twisted on the spot, stumbling and waving his arms as the rodents swarmed around him. Heidi came running out as well, with Max at her ankles. They flung their elf clothes to the ground and jumped on the back of the sledge.

"Go!" she yelled.

Frankie gave the reins a tug. The sledge jolted forwards. He pulled to one side and the mice steered away from the stable. He directed them down the slope.

The mice shot down the hill. Glancing black, Frankie saw that Hans had leapt on to his rat. "Stop them!" he yelled.

Frankie gripped the reins as the sledge bounced across the ground. Sweets were falling off the back and scattering in the snow, and his friends clutched each other tight. "Go, Frankie!" shouted Heidi. "Faster!"

In the distance he saw thick banks of mist, and guessed it must be coming from the lake. They were almost there. As they shot over a small rise, the football rolled out from under his foot towards the edge of the sledge. His pulse spiked in panic. *No ...*

Max's paw stopped it before it was lost.

"Good save!" said Louise.

"Yeah, not bad," said Charlie. "For a dog."

Frankie steered the sledge down a gulley towards the lake's edge. Looking over his shoulder, he couldn't see Hans, but he could hear the rat's bell echoing in the distance. The only light came from the moon above.

The surface of the lake was frozen, and covered in a layer of snow. He slowed the mice with a pull on the reins. Their breath made white clouds on the air.

"Why are you stopping?" asked Max.

"There's no telling how thick the ice is," said Frankie, jumping down from the sledge. "We can't risk taking the sledge."

"OK, let's walk," said Louise, joining him.

Charlie stared towards the thick mist. "Let's hope Gustav was right."

"Ha! Got you!" called Hans, appearing above them on the slope. "I knew you were trouble from the moment I laid eyes on you." His lumbering rat began to descend towards them.

Frankie stepped on to the icy surface of the lake. To his relief, it supported his weight. The others followed.

"Don't be foolish," said Hans, as several other elves drew up alongside him. "There's nowhere to go — the ice is thick at the edges, but in the centre it hasn't been frozen for many years."

Frankie and his friends continued away from the shore, into the mist. Hans slid off his rat and watched.

Then Frankie heard a creaking sound and stopped.

"Hans isn't lying," said Louise. As she shifted her foot, Frankie felt the ice move under his feet. Fear crept across his skin.

"No one move," he said.

Hans was grinning. "Why don't you come back?" he said. "You could be happy in elf world."

Frankie knew he wasn't right.
He wanted to be back with his
mum and dad — even Kevin — for
Christmas Day. He shot a glance
at his friends. It was his fault they
were all trapped here.

Looking back into the mist, he
saw the ice thinned to nothing.

After a few more metres, black water waited to swallow them up. Beyond that, there was only mist. *Elf* mist. He wondered how near they'd got to home.

Not near enough, he thought desperately. He'd let his team down.

"I'm sorry, guys," he said. "I think it's all over."

CHAPTER 8

"Not necessarily," said Louise, nodding at the magic football in Charlie's arms. "All we need is a bit of magic."

"How can it help us now?" asked Heidi.

"I'm not sure," Lou muttered. "But we can only try."

Frankie held out his hands and Charlie tossed the ball to him. He'd trusted the football to get Gustav home. *Time to put my faith in it again.*

"Are you going to stay out there all night?" called Hans.

Frankie placed the football on the ice. "Don't fail me now," he whispered.

He side-footed the ball towards the open water, wondering if he'd ever see it again.

But as it skimmed across the surface, it left a trail of white frost. And instead of sinking into the depths, the water froze beneath it, forming an icy pathway. The ball rolled on into the mist and out of sight.

"Come on!" he said. "It might not last."

With hard ice underfoot, they ran in single file, plunging into the thick fog. Frankie had to push his fear away – just a metre each side, the water was unfrozen. One slip and they'd never get out again. Soon he reached the ball, and gave it another kick. The ice formed a bridge once more, guiding them onward. He was just beginning to feel comfortable when he heard the pounding of footsteps at the rear.

"Hans isn't giving up," said Louise.

They stopped and looked back.

The elf was coming through the mist. "You can't go back!" he shouted.

"We told you," Frankie called back. "Your secret is safe with us."

They heard a loud crack and Hans stopped dead. His mouth became a silent "O" and he looked at his feet. Thin cracks were spreading from where he stood.

Hans took another step. The cracks widened. With a crunch, the ice gave way and Hans dropped through into the water. His cry cut short with a splash.

A moment later he came up, spluttering, and managed to haul

himself out. His face was turning blue. The ice between them had broken apart. Hans couldn't stop them now. They were safe.

Frankie felt a bit sorry for the elf, dripping and shivering. "I promise we won't tell anyone what we've seen," he said.

Hans cursed them as he walked back towards the far shore.

Frankie gave the magic football another kick, and they followed it through the mist. Soon it began to thin, and Frankie didn't need the football any more because the water was already frozen. He saw lights ahead – the windows of the chalets set against the mountainside. They found themselves on the shoreline of a lake, under a moonlit sky.

Thank goodness, he thought. *We're home.*

"Everything's back to normal," he said.

"I don't think so," said Max. "Don't you think it all looks a little ... big?"

It took Frankie a while to understand why.

"We're still tiny!" he said.

Something huge loomed above them. It was a rowing boat, stuck in the ice.

"We need to get one of the
Christmas biscuits," said Louise.
"Otherwise there'll be a lot of
explaining to do."

"My house is about fifty metres
up that hill," said Heidi. "We'd
better get trekking!"

Luckily, there was no one about. Frankie guessed it was sometime in the early hours. Still dark, but maybe not for long. It took for ever to reach the chalet, and they were all puffing by the time they got there.

"What now?" said Charlie. "We can hardly just knock. Our parents will go barmy!"

"Let's go round the back," said Louise. "We can use the cat flap."

As they edged around the towering walls of the chalet, Heidi spoke. "The vanilla biscuits will be hanging from the tree like every Christmas," she said. "Funny, we used to say we put them there to stop the naughty elves reaching them!"

As soon as Frankie saw the cat flap, he realised it was too high up. Even when he jumped, he couldn't reach the rim.

"Stand on my shoulders," said Charlie, crouching down.

Frankie climbed on, and Charlie stood up, wobbling back and forth. Frankie managed to hook a hand over the cat flap, and hauled himself up, so he was sitting across it. Louise came next, then Heidi. Last of all, they reached down and grabbed Charlie's wrists. "How about that for teamwork!" said Frankie.

One by one, they dropped down on the other side.

Frankie could hear voices.

"Kevin, slow down," his mum was saying. "You're not making any sense. Get another blanket, someone. I think he might have hypothermia."

"I'm fine!" said Kevin. "Apart from my ankle, anyway. Listen, there was this elf — his name was Gus or something. They went outside with him ..."

There was a light coming from under the living room door.

Next it was Heidi's brother who spoke. "They've probably returned to the cabin by now, but the phone isn't working. I will walk down there."

"I'll come with you," said Frankie's dad.

"And if they're not there?" asked Heidi's mum.

"Then we will have to fetch the mountain rescue."

Frankie heard footsteps, and he bundled his friends behind a shoe-rack. Moments later, both dads strode past with Marc, looking like giants. They put on their coats and headed out of the back door into the snow.

Charlie groaned. "We're in *so* much trouble."

CHAPTER 9

Frankie and the others crept along the wall to the living room door, which was slightly ajar.
"The mountain rescue won't help them," cried Kevin. "They've been kidnapped by an evil elf!"

"Just lie back," said Frankie's mum. "You're delirious."

Frankie peered around the edge. A fire was roaring in the hearth, and both mums were wearing their dressing gowns. The lights of the Christmas tree twinkled, and a large pile of presents sat at the bottom.

A perfect Christmas, thought Frankie, *apart from being shrunk to the size of a tin of soup.*

Kevin was lying on the sofa, covered by blankets, with a hot water bottle clutched to his chest. "Mum," he said. "If Frankie doesn't come back, can I have his comics?"

"Don't talk like that," replied his mum. "Frankie's a sensible boy – and he's got Louise and Charlie with him. They're probably at the cabin right now."

Kevin smiled to himself. "Could I have another drink please?" he whimpered. "My insides feel cold."

"Of course, darling," said his mum, heading towards the kitchen.

He's loving this, thought Frankie. *Well, he's not getting his hands on my stuff.*

It was just Kevin and Heidi's mum left in the living room. Kevin was looking the other way, and Heidi's mum was shifting logs in the fire with a poker. Frankie beckoned the others after him and scurried from the door to an armchair. Heidi tapped his shoulder and pointed to the tree.

"There are the biscuits," she whispered. "The *vanillekipferl*."

Frankie spotted them, wrapped in brown paper, hanging from the branches. He counted about ten, but even the lowest was nearly half a metre off the ground. Even standing on Charlie's shoulders, he couldn't reach it.

"I don't fancy trying to climb," said Charlie. "It looks very prickly!"

But Frankie had other ideas. The answer was in his rucksack.

"Stay out of sight," he said.

He headed from the armchair, under the coffee table, then stopped as Heidi's mum stood up.

"I must go and fetch more firewood from the log pile," she said.

"Before you go, can I have the remote control, please?" said Kevin.

Heidi's mum handed it to him. Frankie waited until she had left the room, then tiptoed towards the stacks of gifts under the tree. They looked like huge, brightly coloured boulders. Kevin had switched on the TV, and began to flick through the channels. Frankie could see the others huddled together, watching his every move.

He clambered over a red present, using a ribbon to haul himself up

like a rock climber. He spied the gift
tag as he passed:

*Merry Christmas to my wonderful
husband. Please put up those
shelves in the garage xxx*

He grinned. Definitely a DIY
book for his dad.

Frankie hopped across to
a squishy present. The paper
crunched under his feet, and he
froze, expecting Kevin to jump up.
But his brother's eyes were fixed on
the telly.

Frankie glanced up. The nearest
biscuit was way above him,
hanging on a thread. He slipped
off the rucksack and took out the

football. His aim would have to be perfect.

Frankie took a deep breath and tossed the ball up, then booted it as hard as he could straight into the air. It skimmed past the biscuit, making it spin, but then dropped again. Frankie caught it.

"What was that?" said Kevin. Through a gap, Frankie saw his brother rising from the sofa, a frown creasing his forehead. The tree was still wobbling. "I bet it's one of those elves!" said Kevin. He was moving closer. "Come out, little fella — I won't hurt you."

Frankie had nowhere to hide.

His brother closed in, then suddenly squealed in fright and leapt into the air. "Mouse!" Kevin scrambled up on to the sofa. Frankie saw Max scurry under a sofa. *Good work, boy!*

Frankie took his chance, aiming the ball again. This time it hit the biscuit, knocking it off the

branch. Frankie dived out of the way as it came plummeting down. Forgetting the ball, he grabbed it in both arms, and climbed down from the present pile. His brother's shouts had brought both mums running.

"Kevin, what *are* you doing?" said Frankie's mum.

Kevin paused. "I saw a mouse."

"I don't think so," Heidi's mum said. "We have a cat, Kevin."

Kevin climbed down from the sofa.

Frankie couldn't see the others anywhere, until the leaves of a pot plant across the room stirred. Heidi peered out from the other side, then led the others towards her bedroom door and slipped inside.

Frankie quickly followed them, keeping close to the walls.

Heidi's room was cast in shadow with the lights off. Her bunkbed loomed high above them. Two more camp beds lay on the floor.

"You first," said Frankie, unwrapping the biscuit. "This had better work."

Heidi broke off the end of the biscuit, and ate it. The others did the same, and Frankie went last. Between them, they barely made a dent. It tasted nice, but a bit dry.

They all stayed exactly the same size.

"You don't think we have to eat the whole thing, do you?" asked Charlie. "I mean, I love biscuits, but I think we'll struggle."

"Maybe it takes time," said Louise. "We should just stay in here where it's ..." She trailed off, eyes on Heidi's bed. Her face had gone pale.

Max growled.

Frankie's blood ran cold as he saw a monster rising from the bedclothes. A monster covered in thick grey fur, with green eyes. It arched its spine, hissing.

Heidi's cat!

CHAPTER 10

"Hey, Carla," said Heidi. "It's me!"

But Carla either didn't hear or didn't recognise her owner. *We probably look like tasty mice to her,* thought Frankie.

"That's one big cat," said Max, tail drooping between his legs.

Carla leapt from the bed in a graceful bound. Her unblinking eyes watched them hungrily.

Frankie searched for a hiding place, but there was nothing in sight. They'd never be able to outrun a cat, anyway. Carla paced towards them, claws rattling on the wooden floor. Frankie had faced lions, dinosaurs, aliens and sharp-shooting cowboys, but nothing as terrifying as this cat.

"You guys run for it," he said, standing his ground. Carla licked her long white teeth.

I hope this is quick, thought Frankie, holding his breath.

Carla's hind legs bunched, ready to pounce.

But instead she simply sat back, purring. Frankie breathed out. He turned around to see where the others had got to, and saw only huge shoes. His eyes travelled upwards. Charlie, Louise and Heidi were giants!

"Where's Frankie?" said Louise.

He felt a strange lightness in his stomach, as if he was a balloon, expanding. The room began to shrink around him, and he rose through the air. But somehow he still felt the floor beneath his feet. Soon he was level with his friends, and they were all grinning wildly. Carla rubbed her body up against his legs. The biscuit had worked! They were back to normal size.

"She was about to eat us a few seconds ago," said Louise.

"That's why I prefer dogs!" said Frankie. He looked round for Max, but his pet had vanished. *Back to grandma's, I guess.* The football's magic was over.

They all jumped as they heard a door slam.

"No luck!" said Marc. "The cabin is empty. We must call out the emergency services."

Frankie's mum gasped. "Oh no!"

"Told you!" said Kevin.

Heidi scooped up Carla, and

looked at Frankie and his friends.
"Shall we?" she asked.

Frankie nodded, and they all
burst from the bedroom.

The others turned to face them,
their mouths gaping.

"What ...?"

"How ...?"

"When ...?"

Kevin looked a little
disappointed. "Oh, you're back."

Frankie did his best fake yawn.
"We got back ages ago," he said.
"Must have fallen asleep."

"In your clothes?" said Marc.

"Skiing's tiring, isn't it?" said
Charlie.

"We didn't think of checking your room, Heidi," said her mum.

Frankie's mum gave him a huge hug. "We were so worried! Kevin said something about ... well, it sounds silly now ... but elves! Christmas elves kidnapping you!"

Kevin's face had gone a shade of beetroot. "I was telling the truth," he said through gritted teeth.

"Maybe he banged his head as well as twisting his ankle," said Louise. "Black slopes can be dangerous, you know."

"Black slopes!" said Marc.

"Didn't he tell you?" said Charlie innocently.

Frankie's parents both glared at Kevin.

"Go easy on him," said Frankie. "We all make mistakes from time to time. I'm sure Kev's learned his lesson."

Kevin started to splutter angrily.

"I suppose it *is* Christmas," said Frankie's dad, wrapping an arm around Kevin's shoulder. "It'll be dawn in a couple of hours. I for one need some sleep after all this excitement."

"Me also," said Heidi's mum. "After all, we don't want to be up when the elves come calling, do we Kevin?"

Everyone laughed. Everyone apart from Kevin.

"What's this?"

She bent down, and straightened up holding Frankie's football, now back to normal size.

"I knew there was something weird going on!" said Kevin.

The parents and Marc all looked at him in confusion.

"It's Frankie's," said his dad sternly. "And he shouldn't have been playing with it indoors."

Frankie grinned. "Sorry, Dad," he said, trying not to smile. "I won't do it again."

"Why on earth bring a football

on a skiing holiday?" muttered his mother.

Frankie smiled to himself. *It's a good job I did.*

The adults all went off to their bedrooms and Kevin stayed on the sofa, sulking. Frankie followed his friends to Heidi's room. He lay the football down beside his pillow, and crawled into his sleeping bag.

"I wonder if we'll ever see Gustav again," asked Heidi.

"I doubt it," Charlie replied. "He'll probably be more careful in future."

Frankie yawned – a real one this

time. "I think Kevin will too. But if he hadn't gone down that black slope, we'd never have had our adventure."

"So maybe it's always worth trying new things?" said Louise.

"That's not really what I meant," said Frankie. "What if we'd become stranded in the elf world?"

"But we didn't," said Charlie. "Team Frankie pulled through, just like always!"

Frankie grinned to himself. *What a night! Floating cable cars, mice the size of horses, magic biscuits ...*

"Merry Christmas everyone," he said.

"Merry Christmas," came three sleepy replies.

ACKNOWLEDGEMENTS

Many thanks to everyone at Hachette Children's Group; Neil Blair, Zoe King, Daniel Teweles and all at The Blair Partnership; Luella Wright for bringing my characters to life; special thanks to Michael Ford for all his wisdom and patience; and to Steve Kutner for being a great friend and for all his help and guidance, not just with the book but with everything.

Turn the page for a sneak peek
at Frankie's next adventure,
Mammoth Maythem,
coming soon . . .

Frankie and his friends are camping in the countryside near an ancient stone circle. When Kevin grabs the magic football, the team chase him to get it back ...

Frankie ran through the sloping meadow, and he could see he was gaining on his brother. Kevin turned back to look, then suddenly fell down, hard, with a cry. The football flew into the air.

Frankie reached the brow of the hill, and found his brother lying on the ground, grimacing and clutching his ankle. He'd tripped over a rock sticking up out of the ground.

"Are you all right?" Frankie asked.

Kevin's face was red and sweating. "I think I've broken it!" he said.

Louise crouched down, and gingerly pushed up Kevin's trouser leg. "It doesn't look broken," she said. "Probably just a sprain. There's some ice back at the campsite."

"Who left that rock there anyway?" said Kevin. He kicked it

grumpily with his other foot.

"Who knows," said Charlie. "But I think it's been there a while."

Frankie saw what he meant. The stone was just one of dozens, all laid out in a huge circle. Some were bigger than others, coming almost up to his waist, while some had fallen over and lay on their sides.

"Looks like we've found the stone circle," he said.

"It's magnificent!" said Louise. "Can you imagine how long they've stood here on this hill? What a magical place!"

"Where's the football?" asked Charlie.

The grass inside the stone circle was quite long, so they all began to search together. Frankie thought it hadn't gone far, but he couldn't find it anywhere. Max trotted this way and that, just his wagging tail showing above the grass.

Suddenly, with a yelp, he dropped out of sight.

"Max?" called Frankie, rushing over. He stopped suddenly. Where Max had been a moment ago, the grass had vanished, leaving only a black hole in the ground. It looked like an open manhole cover, descending into a bottomless abyss.

Frankie recognised a portal when he saw one. The football must have made it.

"Where does it go?" asked his brother.

"Who knows?" said Frankie. "But Max is down there, so I'm going after him."

"Me too!" said Charlie.

"And me," added Louise.

Frankie looked at his friends. "Ready?"

"Ready," they repeated.

They linked hands and jumped into the portal together.

Competition Time

COULD YOU BE A WINNER LIKE FRANKIE?

Every month one lucky fan will win an exclusive
Frankie's Magic Football goodie bag! Here's how to enter:

Every **Frankie's Magic Football** book
features different animals. Go to:
www.frankiesmagicfootball.co.uk/competitions
and name three different animals that feature in three
different **Frankie's Magic Football** books.
Then you could be a winner!

You can also send your entry by post by filling in
the form on the opposite page.

Once complete, please send your entries to:

Frankie's Magic Football Competition
Hachette Children's Books, Carmelite House,
50 Victoria Embankment,
London, EC4Y 0DZ

GOOD LUCK!

Competition Entry Page

Please enter your details below:

1. Name of Frankie Book:
   Animal:

2. Name of Frankie Book:
   Animal:

3. Name of Frankie Book:
   Animal:

My name is:

My date of birth is:

Email address:

Address 1:

Address 2:

Address 3:

County:

Post Code:

Parent/Guardian signature:

FRANKIE'S MAGIC FOOTBALL WEBSITE

Have you had a chance to check out **frankiesmagicfootball.co.uk** yet?

Get involved in **competitions**, find out **news** and **updates** about the series, play **games** and watch **videos** featuring the author, **Frank Lampard!**

Visit the site to join **Frankie's FC** today!